One Caring Kid

A Book About YOU—
and What Your Kindness Can Do!

Written by Michaelene Mundy
Illustrated by R.W. Alley

ONE
CARING
PLACE

Abbey Press
St. Meinrad, IN 47577

To our three caring kids who have grown into three wonderful, caring adults.

Text © 2008 Michaelene Mundy
Illustrations © 2008 Saint Meinrad Archabbey
Published by One Caring Place
Abbey Press
St. Meinrad, Indiana 47577

Library of Congress Catalog Number
2007909719

ISBN 978-0-87029-414-3

Printed in the United States of America

A Message to Parents, Teachers, and Other Caring Adults

We may think that *caring* comes naturally to kids. They haven't become skeptics like so many of us. Not having the financial expectations and burdens that we adults have, they often genuinely want to reach out unselfishly to help others. However, there is no question that caring is also very much a learned virtue, one that we can model and teach. It is a virtue that children can carry within and pass on to the people they come into contact with throughout their lives. Wise people say that caring is not taught very much at all, but is caught.

In either case, we want our children to be nice, kind, loving, and caring in all instances. This book is meant to inspire us adults to pass on virtues we may have forgotten that we have within ourselves.

In focusing on a child's actions rather than the child himself, we allow our children to affirm themselves. What they do is nice, kind, thoughtful rather than they are nice, kind, thoughtful. Children can mistrust us telling them that they are good because we are "supposed" to do that. We would like them to "discover" they are nice.

Can one person, and particularly a child, really make a difference? Is it only important to be kind to people and say please and thank you when you really mean it? What does our religion, our faith, our society tell/teach us about caring?

Hopefully this book responds to these questions. The thoughts and ideas are intended to give children and adults simple guidance. It is hoped that this book will also help parents and teachers and other adults experience, and re-learn in some cases, the gifts we gain in showing kindness and caring.

—*Michaelene Mundy*

Sometimes It's Easy to Be Caring

When it's a beautiful day and you're not hungry, and you're not bored, and you're not worried about anything in particular, it's easy to be caring and kind to those around you.

It's easy to smile back at someone on a lovely day. It's easy to smile at someone doing something nice for you—like Dad, as he puts a big stack of pancakes (with lots of syrup) on your plate.

On good days, you could walk around being nice to everyone—even share a favorite toy.

And Sometimes It's Hard to Be Caring

When things aren't going so well—when it rains on the day your family was going to the park, or when your sister plays with one of your toys without asking—it's not so easy to be kind.

Your parents and teachers tell you that you must try to be kind ALL the time, not just when it is easy. They tell you to "love your enemies" and you shouldn't hate anyone or anything. That's hard to do on bad days. What would it be like if everyone cared about each other—not just a friend or someone you LIKE, but everyone and everything that God made?

Caring About the People You Already Know

Sometimes it can even be hard to care about people you know. After all, you know good things AND not-so-good things about them. Living with people, spending time with them, lets us see them on their good AND bad days.

You know how much fun your friend is when you play a board game together. You probably also know that when the game is over, she never helps put the game pieces away.

Your brother may be great at playing the piano, but sometimes he plays too loud when you are watching TV or reading a book.

Caring About People You Don't Know

Think about a really good friend. Try to remember what your friend was like before you really got to be good friends.

Everyone wonders what people are like until they get to know them. Someone may be wondering what kind of a friend you would be.

But all the people in the world really belong to one, big family...God's family. It is good to get to KNOW each other, even if that means just hearing about other places and the people who live there and how they are the same as you and different than you. Could you get along with these people?

Caring About Yourself

Parents and teachers may tell you that you *should* care about others. But first you must REALLY care about yourself. God wants us to be kind to others and God wants us to be kind to ourselves, too.

Have you ever said or thought, "I am so stupid," because of a silly thing you did? Instead, try to recall that what you *did* may have been silly or stupid, but *you* are not stupid.

A wise person once said: "You better like yourself—because that is the person you spend the most time with!" So true!

Caring About Our World

When you see the news on TV about your world, you can feel really small and not very important. You may feel that there are so many wars, accidents, and other bad things that you can't do anything to make the world better.

But when you do just one good thing, you have made the world better for someone.

You can treat the whole world with one kindness after another. You could become a pen-pal to someone far away. Not only can you share good things with them, you will gain good things, too. You will see how we are alike in so many ways and that differences can be good.

Caring About God

God wants your love and care, too. How can you love God when you hardly know much more about God than you know about a stranger?

You need to get to know God. Listening to what your parents and teachers tell you about God will help you get to know God. You can hear about God as you listen to stories at church that tell about God's kindness and care.

God cares about YOU—when things are good, when things are bad, when things are in-between good and bad. This is what God hopes YOU can do toward others.

Forgiving Is the Caring Thing

There are some things in the world that are perfect—butterflies, smiling babies, your grandma's hug.

Most things in life are not perfect, including people. People can hurt each other a lot...with actions and words. In order to get along—even when someone hurts you—it is important that you learn to forgive. AND there will be times when you need to be able to ask others to forgive you when you hurt them.

Forgiveness means being able to say to yourself and to others: "Nobody is perfect. Let's not stay mad at each other. Let's find a way to get along."

Kindness Can Be Catching/Contagious

Usually you think of "catching" as something you do with a ball—or maybe catching something contagious…like a cold. Kindness is catching and contagious, too.

If your baby sister sees you poking or shoving the dog, she will probably start poking or shoving the dog, too. If your baby brother sees you being kind or doing something nice, he just might do the same thing, too.

If enough people do nice things, and if enough people "copy" them, think of the kinder, more loving world we would live in. (And think how happy all the dogs might be, too.)

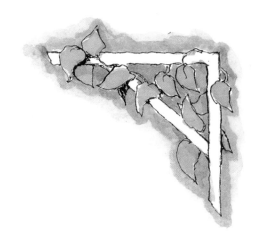

Let God Do Some of the Caring, Too

To see and hear about all the problems around us, you might wonder if God really cares about people and things in the world. Some problems are so big that ONLY God can take care of them.

You are needed to do your part to help God. One way to help God is to trust God. When you say your prayers, you are telling God that you are leaving the REALLY hard parts to God. But you can also promise God that you will keep praying and that you will keep doing your own special part to help.

Change the World– Start With You

You'd probably like all the big AND little problems in the world fixed. When you see litter on the sidewalk, you may wish people wouldn't drop things for someone else to pick up. Your brother may make loud noises when he eats and you wish he would stop. Do these people not CARE?

Sometimes, you can't do much about what other people think or do. What you CAN do a lot about is what YOU think or do.

Have you heard the song "Let There Be Peace on Earth?" The song says "and let it begin with me." You can begin, even inside yourself, to make the world better.

Having the Courage to Care

Really caring sometimes means being brave and standing up for what is right or speaking up when you see someone doing something wrong.

Your friend may not like it when you tell her that people can't hear the movie well when she talks too loud in a theater. Your neighbor won't like it when you tell him to stop being mean to a cat or dog. Speaking up can make a difference, but you need to be brave to do it.

The word "courage" comes from an ancient word meaning "heart." You show you have a heart, when you show courage in speaking up.

Remember Your Heroes

You already know some really kind people and you have heard or read about many more.

Maybe you have an aunt who is very busy, but she stops what she is doing to look at every page of your scrapbook. Maybe your hero is Mother Teresa, who cared for the poorest and least "wanted" people in the world, especially when they were sick and dying.

As you grow up, what kind and loving person do YOU want to be like? You can be someone's hero, too. You can even be someone's hero NOW. Ordinary people can be heroes when they are loving and kind.

Listen to Your Heart

Love and care: these two things seem to take care of almost every problem. The world NEEDS love and care. The good news is, you can give the world something it needs.

Listen to what your heart tells you to do. Ask yourself, "What is the loving thing to do?" when you see someone sad or worried.

You may never know just how much you have changed the world because of something as simple as smiling at another person on the street. But you can make a difference…one little smile at a time!

Michaelene Mundy is the author of a number of Elf-help Books for Kids, including the top-selling *Sad Isn't Bad* and *Mad Isn't Bad*. She holds advanced degrees in community and school counseling and has raised three children. She began her career as an elementary school teacher and now counsels high school students.

R. W. Alley is the illustrator for the popular Abbey Press adult series of Elf-help books, as well as an illustrator and writer of children's books. He lives in Barrington, Rhode Island, with his wife, daughter, and son. See a wide variety of his works at: www.rwalley.com.